— *The* —
APPALACHIAN
SEA

SOUTHERN MESSENGER POETS

Dave Smith, Series Editor

The — APPALACHIAN SEA

POEMS

STEVE SCAFIDI

Louisiana State University Press

Baton Rouge

Published by Louisiana State University Press

lsupress.org

LSU Press Paperback Original

DESIGNER: Michelle A. Neustrom
TYPEFACE: Bembo MT Pro

COVER ILLUSTRATION: *Creature*, 2024, by Miles Cleveland Goodwin.
Courtesy of the artist.

Cataloging-in-Publication Data are available from the Library of Congress.

ISBN 978-0-8071-8471-4 (paperback) | ISBN 978-0-8071-8513-1 (epub) |
ISBN 978-0-8071-8514-8 (pdf)

For Norman Dubie
1945–2023

~~~~~~~~

The winter comes,
A sea hunting . . .

Contents

The

APPALACHIAN SEA

On the Occasion of a Black Horse and the New Life

I'd just read Whitman out loud the first time and gone
 To sleep and dreamed, a teenager in his miseries,
And after a while something started to happen.
 After pushing the fence down, the black horse bright
In the moonlight started up the path followed by Thelma
 The mule followed by Darby the donkey followed by Puff-
Puff the old unshorn sheep fat as a cloud in
 The night sky, and their hooves going startled me
Awake while house-sitting at my friend's farm.
 I knew this ritual, walking like a pilgrim in the dark
With an offering. They knew I was a stranger and went.
 I gathered a bowl of oats and followed them in the night
Down the road hoping no cars full of drunks zipped by,
 Hoping I could find them but they went slow clip-clopping
In the moonlight, so I saw and heard as they turned
 Under the trees down a neighbor's lane—a train of going
And not caring really, so I found them grazing at three
 In the morning in the front yard of the neighbor's house
The four of them peacefully grazing together by the door,
 The windows darkened as they stood there the four of them
Friends or allies at least, silhouettes against the place
 Darkened down for sleep, and I shook my bowl of oats and so
They followed me wanting to be home and to eat the oats
 That were golden and something of magnificence in light,
Wanting to show me this lovely new way through the hours.

Of Red Earth and Old Love

In the winter pasture just north of the pond far away
  From the house, down the hill so the road cannot see—
There is a cut in the field like a grave and flames
  Rise from it and lick at all times. Oil from the Mesozoic.
Hell-gate. The grave of some grandfather who was a bastard.
  We don't know but it barely smokes and makes only a
Glow, a crimson glow low on the horizon if you look out
  From an upper window in the farmhouse. Like a bonfire
Way off for some bride and groom you've never met, some
  Celebration of good tidings. Or an undiscovered volcano
Asleep under the hill. We go there on winter nights
  For the calm and the mystery for it is not always a story
Of good and evil when something happens and no one is hurt
  And no one understands. It is a thing before you: a dog
Born with two heads. A child doing calculus at the table.
  An ordinary woman or an ordinary man just waking up
In the world looking about, worried and happy and utterly
  Unknowing what is about to come over the hill. We look
At each other after all these years and here we are—still
  Together living near some mysterious underground flame.

Spoon Chimes

Arthritis bends and warps the fingers like splayed
    Boards left out in the sun and the rain and they
Hurt and you stir the milk into your coffee
    With a straight decorative spoon very lightly
So the chime is one-two, one-two, and that's it.
    I don't remember you otherwise. I don't remember
Your stories, the sound of your voice, if you had lost
    Loves, of course, or flew a kite made of newspaper
In the pasture a hundred years ago. Maybe. I just guess
    At you and who you were and the dairy cow probably
Who was your friend, or the raccoon you tamed
    Who followed you to school. I remember your crooked
Fingers somehow holding a spoon straight and stirring
    Easily and the tiny bell that filled the room. How many
Of us will enter the oblivion of our loved one's
    Lives in a hundred years or less? Probably most of us.
You knew. You knew this and we clinked glasses, I think,
    One drinking coffee and one drinking milk at the table,
A boy and a dead man on the day before it was official.

The First of September in Summit Point

Auden was right after all: we must love one another
   And die, and learning to do the first helps with learning
The other. One time a boy told his friends he was
   Going to kill himself and ran outside into the summer
Night and his friends took off after him through the dark
   Orchard behind the house calling for him and running, going
Sorrow-mad with looking while the quarter moon hung up
   Above the great sycamore in the orchard, a landmark
Huge and towering over the apple trees, they called the Peace
   Tree which was a common meeting place for teenagers
Who were friends escaping their homes to roam the night
   Having their fun. And the orchard was poisoned last year,
The trees piled up and set aflame as bonfires huge
   As houses at wartime although the sycamore remains
Even now, unharmed, surrounded by cornfield instead
   Of apples. Its silver nude a thing of beauty towering there
In the orchard that is now invisible behind the town
   Where my son and his friends found their friend at
Last and told him they loved him and stayed the night
   Keeping close by him, all of them still catching their breath,
All of them still catching their breath on the changing land.

Near the Holy Cross Abbey

That tall shy man flying through the air
　　Leaping from the riverside
To coast above the water—
　　And his bride also,
Slowly flying just behind him—
　　Were two blue herons
At the beginning of the world
　　It seems. We disturbed them
From their eggs and their peace.
　　A Tuesday at springtime
In the new century, much
　　Like the last. *Don't worry,*
We're leaving—come back.

Of a Long Life

It seems rare to travel great distances like this.

   The train moves out and goes and the conductor

Finds us where we are, helps us out and gets

   Us to where we need and the uniform is polite

And clean. Going to Sacramento, ok. To Duluth,

   Alright come on. In the last days of her mother's

Life she pantomimed giving her ticket to whoever

   Was there, waiting for someone to stamp it, take it

Gently from her hand and say there you go and so

   Assure her. We took it from her for three long days

While it snowed sideways out the hospital window.

   And the snow fell through her eyes—opaque,

Open to whatever she saw in or out of them:

   Lake Superior in 1943, her father walking

Into the water with her astride his shoulders.

   His jet-black hair she held to as they went

Under a moment and rose again to the blue of sky

   Like his eyes and her mother's kerchief on her head

Up on the beach. Which she focused on

   As she left the room and the snow stopped.

Elegy for Bob Lanham, Who Made the Hay

The yellow hill before you rising like a wave with another
   Larger hill rising behind it is the vantage point
Here at the edge of some woods, hay field behind hay
   Field in February, the serene nothing of the last mowing
Showing the hills close to the bone. Just the geology
   Of rising and falling with the stubble of hay and no
Cattle, no sheep, no man, no fence, no house, no barn
   No horses, only the hills in February, two of them like waves
Rising golden with a hint of green because of the rain—
   Some promise of heat coming on, the growing of timothy,
The work we love. *The work we love* is such a tricky phrase
   Anymore for why must we love our work and not simply
Do it and move on? My friend Bob died a few years ago
   As an old man but when he was young he reached across
The blades of the corn-cutter and cut off his hand at
   The wrist and drove to the hospital woozy and angry
Raving a little nearly bleeding out though he lived,
   His steel hook swinging at the end of his arm for years.
He loved bush-hogging, doing hay and cutting corn
   And was happy out there alone in the rising fields,
Cussing underneath the sun and he'd say you're full of it,
   Motherfucker, you're entirely and truly full of shit as ever.

By a Country Church

One way or another he is always out there either
    Sniffing at the foundations with his cloak and long tail
And claws crouching by the door. Or wearing the simple
    Cover of a suit and tie as the visiting preacher with
Something old to say. On the tv news of the hurricane
    He is just slightly visible in the window of the warehouse.
At dinner he is father, often daddy, murderous-eyed
    Ready to jump. Or mother come to really show you this time,
The lock clicked shut for days. Mostly though he moves
    Like a ruminant, some beast of a dairy cow gentle
Through your mind, grazing shaking that colossal head
    And horns slowly so the bell rings, that perpetual Nothing
Who says you should be dead, should go ahead, coward
    Do it, lily-livered little slutty little creep everyone
Hates you for god's sake wake up, wake up and see
    The horror you are by being, the voice in your head we all
Listen to sometimes just ordinary moving along the green
    Hills inside you, making that poisoned milk we love.

Thistles on Seven Hills Farm

After Mr. Leonard died and his land was abandoned
   I remember seeing acres of thistles each as tall
As a man, as if an army stood before us quietly
   Like the funerary army of that Chinese emperor
Buried with his treasures and the terracotta ghosts
   Of 200 BC, those clay soldiers each fashioned
After a living soul, so the tall purple flowers stood
   Everywhere with thorns and a thousand quick birds
Darting and this was the in-between period after
   The farmer died and his lands lay abandoned after
Corn and soybean and corn and wheat and hay and
   Thistles now by the thousands standing together before
All is sold and houses rise up and the people come to
   Stay and thistle has a milky blood when you cut it
Down and it bleeds as if that thick milk courses
   Through its body at all times and so I praise those tall
Guardians of a time now gone who rose up suddenly
   At the death of a man who worked this place with
A blade in the dark earth which he has entered now
   As we will enter the earth eventually on our own,
Never to be so well remembered or to be seen again.

Of Haints in the Woods

It was night-time in the dream and my three-year-old girl
   Ran out of the woods by the house and into the moonlit
Yard and I was in the window upstairs watching as another
   Isabella ran out of the woods laughing and suddenly
Another of her identical, the three of them like sisters,
   Held hands in a circle and the image of their dancing
And the sound of their singing together as one was so
   Unnerving I have never forgotten after twenty years.
Who are we seeing when the people we love run out
   Of the woods suddenly in the dark like this? Who is it
Talking to us on the phone whose voice is so garbled, so
   Low it's a mumble because he has been dead for years?
Who is that woman when I was a boy only dreaming, who
   Stood under a tree and called to me walking toward me
Slowly her eyes full of x's as she approached? Who
   Am I to see all of this, to write the details down, these
Stories from another world? My daughter says to relax,
   It's just that old carnival wheel turning inside us and
Anyway you are a writer and are supposed to see things
   The real and the unreal in everything and she is right.
Just under my skin, the skeleton so quiet and dignified
   Just waiting in the body, just biding its time to be free
At the edge of some woods in the middle of the night.

Mending the Gates

Between the underworld that is the unconscious
    Of a man and the daylight. Between
The waking and the sound asleep. Between your love
    And you. Your body and the pinwheeling
Flicker of the mind that moves us. Between Virginia
    And West Virginia I have always lived, never
Entirely of one place or another. Of my right mind
    And some lost tropic of Being that is a trance
Really of seeing. And between your father and your mother
    You have come to greet the world the same as me.
Between us these words. A man in overalls dingy worn
    Old and also wearing an orange shirt hammers
Together the old boards of a gate so everything will stay
    Safe somehow, keep to its side or gently pass through.
He is a farmer in a field of golden hay near the river
    And has been at this work since the early days
Even before the Bronze Age at the temple, leading in
    The huge bull with horns to be sacrificed,
Always shooing flies from his face, always tending to him
    So he will provide for the gods a proper gift—
To mend the broken passage between us who live here
    Lonely and desperate for a blessing on the earth.

When I Was a Dog and It Was Summer

When it was late August and the air was dust
   And shadow on the water and green light
I loved a person in a way that is common
   Among dogs, especially the Spaniels who hunt,
Who bring and care for and listen and do what
   Is called for. The person I loved called for me
And I appeared is how it seemed. In the woods,
   Along the hills by the house, in the cool mosses
And the curling stream. I never knew about
   The stars until I was grown, never looked up
To the sky for gods or from despair. I ran
   Alongside what charmed me and living
Was like a secret world uncovered. Enchanted,
   Singing, I ranged the world beside this person
Who was specific, particular as any sycamore
   With white bark and blue bark and crazy figures
Climbing into the heavens. And I have kept her
   In my mind—this woman whose perfume was
The word *always* and the way it shimmers
   When you say it so it clings to you a little like
The earth when you roll around in it. Even now
   She watches as I swim in Indian Creek and cool.

A Mangled Bird in the Moss

The woodpeckers of John Jay Audubon's painting
    Gabble and talk on a branch and are sisters
Or close friends for sure, hardly looking around but here,
    At peace, eating the ants they found in the blue sky
Branches of a dead tree. The red-headed noble
    Birds at rest, in company, and this was just before
One was shot, painted, and eaten by the artist
    In a stew with carrots and onions he traded coins
For with a Shawnee man in the woods. He didn't paint
    The mangled bird in the moss, only one that no longer
Existed up in the trees at peace with her sisters.
    He didn't paint the broken wings snapped like twigs
From the fall or the force of the birdshot that tore at
    The group he painted later in their happiness.
He painted what he destroyed although he was
    A naturalist, though a painting of death, of a killed bird
Bleeding in the moss is more true. Like the funeral
    Pictures of children from the nineteenth century dressed
For church seated in a rocking chair in the parlor,
    Their closed eyes and the grimace of their absence
Shows the lie. *Yes I looked a little something like this,*
    Look—these were my ribbons when I was alive.

Of Henrietta Going By

He pulled her in a wagon through town,
   A child's wagon with pillows and blankets,
His older sister whose legs were gone,
   Whose mind was slowed to a resting point
So she saw you, saw your house and looked
   As she was pulled toward the post office or
Her cousin's house, the old man bent never
   Talking, strong, leaning into his direction.
When it rained, in the snow or on the burning
   August road. We rarely spoke and they
Disappeared years ago to death or the State
   Infirmary, but I remember Henrietta held a small
Mirror out as she went, a compact for a lady's
   Make-up, and she looked at the back like it was
A telescope at me as she passed, my world
   So blurry in the glimpse as if down a well.

That Feeling the World Is Ending

The gods in Autumn go their separate ways:
    Of the Trees to flying and to falling underground,
Of the Hay to within themselves and away,
    Of Dogs toward fires and whatever remains
Running quick through the field when it's cold.
    Of Men—anywhere where it is safe and warm.
Why have You left us here with those
    Who want to kill us or want to hunt us down?
What happens now that we are on our own?
    He knows the laughter of a woman in a green dress.
She was his mother in her window in September
    While he walked toward the house with a snake
In each hand. Rat snakes for the cellar
    She asked him to catch. Norman will learn soon
How to fly in his mind everywhere he wants to go
    Even here to this memory. The countryside now is
The red color of her throat when she was just
    Laughing at a boy. Who lived a long time it turns
Out, only just now dying an old man in Arizona,
    A writer I loved. Everything is about to end it seems,
Like poetry, people say, and yet here we are. Here we are.

Short Hill Mountain Doorway

Every springtime the clatter of tools being
   Gathered and carried and a new sense of loss.
All of the bees flying half-drunk with life,
   And all these old men shooting themselves
Along the mountainside as the snow melts.

   All these men searching for the way under
Ground to their deaths and some great hall
   With torches where their fathers' shadows
Might flicker and how they rush to join them.

   These four dead farmers by the river, one
Broken from falling off a ladder, and one
   Diagnosed with blood cancer again, another
By the loss of his son, and one shot through
   With debt to drain all he was. The variations
Are well known. These men dead and gone,
   The cedar buds copper, the daffodils high.
The old mountain door will need to be rebuilt—
   Blown open by gunshot, by despair, their
Blood now making the spring our own. So
   This morning we carry the oak planks up
The path with our hammers and nails and
   The iron hinges for the errand is always to
Make again, to imagine and see what comes
   From what living has racked and blown in.

In Praise of Oblivion

My friend carved a small phoenix from mahogany and it looks
  Like a dragon leaping into the air, its fine feathers lines
Billy carved carefully so the thing almost flies and you
  Hold it carefully so it won't get away, the long neck
Surging upward and the wings banging the air down
  To the earth, and he got the idea from a carver who lived
In the 18th century in Philadelphia and worked unknown
  Making finial torches of walnut or wild roses of pine
For the grandfather clocks being built, for the tall dressers
  Made in the shops by journeymen capable, little-paid,
Though masters of something real: the made-thing
  That sings. No one knows who they were anymore.
Like the woman chipping at a stone to make beads inside
  A cave on the coast of Spain thousands of years before
Stonehenge and so many amphorae painted with golden
  Bulls leaping in the air and arrowheads everywhere
Along the creeks and streams nearby their angles cut
  For quickness in the air for the bison or the mammoth.
The Great Woolly Mammoth we hunted to extinction
  Some scientists are trying to revive to be born in a lab
Or a zoo and perhaps farmed for meat or our delight,
  The smell of their bodies a musk of acorns and the river
Moving through roots of pawpaw trees and wild cherry
  Here in the Shenandoah where they drank, this small
Herd just resting like boulders in the long silver water.

Of Feeling Upside Down

I once found a young 8-point buck deer hanging
  By a back hoof upside down from a barbed-
Wire fence so high he could not touch the ground
  So swung there until we fired, the blood smell
Deep as we cut him down. I once saw Mussolini
  Upside down in a photo, beaten and shot while people
Picked at the corpse for being a fascist. The carnival
  Once came to town here when we were boys
And Todd climbed aboard the Teacups that twirled
  And the carney started the ride and left and
Disappeared so the town's children spun for an hour
  Puking falling upside down screaming in the twirl
Of the cups in the parking lot. I remember thinking of
  Saint Peter asking to be crucified upside down because
He was unworthy. I remember the audacity of that,
  And the painting where his muscled naked body suffered
The nails and gravity filling his head with blood.
  There is no end to cruelty and accident and death.
Julius Caesar cut off the hands of every man and boy
  In the village of Uxellodunum in Gaul as he conquered
His way to an empire, some of the hands still moving
  By the block and blade, blind holding onto each other.

In Marshes and Deep Woods

In the meadows of Paradise and in the bramble by the gates
    The soul of a rattlesnake curls and rests in the midday sun.
Along the rivers of heaven the vipers float and rest un-
    Perturbed, not interested in biting or snapping or taking down
Anyone to death, being already there and whatever waits just
    After—the cobra leaves her basket and joins her sisters
Under the palms and the mangroves. There used to be a house
    Built mostly underground near a stream and my friend lived there.
With cottonmouths coiled by the bed where it was cool.
    Under the fridge where it was dark. By the toilet where it was
Chilly and damp and peaceful and sometimes on the steps
    Would rest two or three of these snakes my friend always
Caught gently and walked outside in a net. And so
    His days were spent in kindness and in mercy with what
Would kill him easily. He wasn't a saint. He was an asshole
    To my sister and he hurt my friends it seemed for fun. But he
Loved the serpents and protected them and was a brother
    To the reptiles he lived among and died in a car accident
In West Virginia in 2005. The silence of 4 AM always
    Reminds me of him and I don't know why. That silence like
The eerie deep sleep of snakes nearby, always closer than we think.

Being Fifteen

Walking in the woods at night sometimes
   It is easy to lose your way unless
You look up at the path in the sky,
   A kind of reflection or mirror-image
Of the path on earth. The one down
   Low darkens to nothing and so if you
Look up at the lighter dark of the sky
   Surrounded by the darker dark
Of the trees you can see the blue
   Wending-way, way up there going
South a while or to the left and so arrive.
   This is how my friends and I traveled
To each other when we were young
   And no one could see our plans
Or read our minds or tell us how to live,
   Moving through branch-thick woods
Passing between two kinds of light.

Of Bewilderment in Middle Age

Because it was surprising and fun and confounding
   Salvador Dalí had a cigarette case he would open
To offer a friend a little moustache, there being several
   Laid together in different styles neatly in the tin,
Curlicue or brushy or Chaplinesque or thin as his—
   Like wire coiled out from either side of his face.
My father has always had a moustache, something
   Fine to sleep along his upper lip like a caterpillar
In the trees and his father, dashing as Clark Gable,
   Walked around in the world in the style of Clark Gable.
The moustache, the Flavor-Saver, the Titty-Tickler or
   The Horizon-Line, the Squirrel-Tail, the Great M of
The villain from movies tying a damsel to the tracks
   Wearing his cape and high heels and his bouffant
Black as his moustache weighing ten pounds perhaps
   Like a baby walrus on an ice floe just napping with
His mother somewhere in the North Sea. Salvador,
   I think of you as I get older and more strange, more
Unfamiliar to what surrounds me and always has
   My whole life—the trees the houses the roads the sky.
How ordinary and traditional to die in Madrid in 1989.
   How beautiful and sacred it is to ever have lived at all.

The Unlikeliness

A cat and a bird lie down together in the sun to sleep:

   My yellow cat Thomas and a dove on the porch. As if

It is a wolf and a lamb in a sacred book, or the man

   Who beats her and the woman asleep. Someone

Plays the piano on a ship above three miles of dark

   Open sea that heaves to take the sound and beauty

To the bottom. Satan and Jehovah on a cloud

   With dice watch Job bury his wife and his child

And his child and his child for days wearing the blade

   Of his shovel to nothing. Nothing and something

Rushing in. Nothing and the random insistence I am

   A part of, with you even though we are strangers, that

We live, we are still here. It doesn't matter says the cat

   To the bird to the fat slick worm being pulled from

The earth. It doesn't matter says the lamb to the wolf

   Though it does, of course it does. You are my reason for

Living he says and she hears the old purr of his voice

   And remembers, comes close, and buries the knife

In his chest. Sometimes the lesson is learned just in time.

   And sometimes it's not a lesson at all, only what happens

In West Virginia in the house by the road where the river

   Bends almost in a circle it is so continuous toward the sea.

Of a Man Falling from the Sky

Thousands of garter snakes fell from the sky in Memphis

    In 1877 in the mild January that is wintertime

In the South and horses ran through the streets spooked

    By what tangled in their manes, women with parasols

Grimly stepping through the writhing made it home safely

    And no one died or could explain to the poor snakes

What lifted them and spun them around except the wind

    That lifted them and spun them around over the Mississippi

River and the cable cars and the mansions and the shacks,

    Waves of snakes biting the air. My grandmother's chimney

Filled with them and they set out through the house looking

    For the green lights of doors and windows and so it went.

Frogs in Arkansas, locusts in the Bible, iguanas in

    Tallahassee—all events of weather and the unexpected

Like those men and women well dressed in New York City

    That day falling from the flames astonished from despair.

One man unknown we still see hanging there upside down

    In the famous photograph, in the blue September morning

In the sky, to whom I have often asked questions before

    Sleep—not who are you exactly but who are we and what is

Happening to us? You and I so quiet and so still for the moment.

Miss Teen West Virginia Walking By

I saw Miss Teen West Virginia in her white dress, sash, and crown
  Walking out of the Methodist Church next to our house
Yesterday and thought of the weird glory of old things like
  Queens and mountains and beauty and how the dogwoods
Growing everywhere here are starting to die off. Thought
  How fragile everything is and doomed and how depressing
I have become. How Ecclesiastes says baby, live it up.
  There is a time for living and a time for dying so there
Must also be a time for swimming in the Shenandoah and
  Riding a Ferris wheel or drinking honey-wine on a Sunday.
And Miss Teen West Virginia was walking to her car after
  The service, after she shook everyone's hand and smiled
Probably for hours so her face ached, her entourage
  Only her mother and father and her younger brother, all
Of whom helped her climb into the minivan with her
  Regalia and my son said yeah that's Allison who attends
My high school and said yeah she's nice, and we watched them
  Drive away and hoped for the best for her and our state
That likes mostly to destroy itself with killing the mountains
  And keeping the young people down enough to die early
Or leave and my son says *No, that is not true* standing there
  Gently before me, at home, ready for it, all heart and soul.

Of the Image of a Sunfish

One time my friend's father caught a snapping turtle
   So huge it barely fit in the trash can he used
To haul it from the pond across the field calling
   For help to thump gently thump it into the cellar's
Dark where for months he fed it fish and lettuce
   Until it grew fat and fierce and stood in the corner
Of the cellar near the washing machine where
   My friend tip-toed with his basket in his arms past
The great beaked animal staring at him from a corner
   Hissing and getting up quick to see Chris run wild
Upstairs terrified, and down there in the historic dark
   Old as the river and the ponds, she thinks of mud
And sunfish so bright even an old snapper will bite
   And be filled and live a while longer. When his father
Was ready he had to search into the darker smaller
   Regions under the house with a flashlight crawling
Calling to her now grown stronger over the summer
   And looked behind him as she came toward him under
The pine joists angry and ready, the struggle going on
   Just below my friend who heard the machete banging
Against the floor under the house as if under the world,
   As if in dream, everything tender seeming soaked in blood.

By the Garden

Because we are older now and trying to savor
    What is left of who we are on the earth,
Every Friday I visit with my parents
    And my mother cooks dinner so good
We close our eyes in the steam.
    Chicken pot pie, potatoes, and carrots,
A salad of greens, a small bowl of
    Strawberries. Sometimes happiness comes
And radiates like that bliss in half-sleep
    When you discover a kind of perfect rest
Going on, on-going in your bones. It is
    Possible, such things, I try to remember.
Out the window behind my father's ear:
    Daylilies and daylilies and daylilies.

Elegy for the Hammer and Anvil Farm

About the melted gas can flung by the house, about the dead

    Farmer and his land being sold and the great burn pile

His daughter started and the explosion heard from town?

    It was that sawed-off little fucker, Bunky, a friend

To Mary Anne who started flinging gas on the burn-pile

    While it was already in flames, that laughing jackass

With his hat backwards who got the bomb in his hands

    Falling and rolling all over funny as shit to be honest.

Let him burn I thought. Let him climb the air as a spiral

    And be elegant for once meeting the Tuesday night clouds

Like a ghost. But no, he was fine and laughed about it

    But he was scared and you could see the bullshit of his

Life reduced to silence and guff as he jerked around

    On the ground and no one laughed but me and Mary Anne

And anyway who cares? The redbud and ailanthus are gone,

    Cut stacked or burned away proper in the bonfire we made,

All that grew around everywhere when her father died.

    His stained-glass studio now home to raccoons wandering

The crimson and cerulean shards, shitting on everything, might

    As well burn that down too, might as well save nothing at all

Of those we loved and who are gone. Is what I was thinking

    Before I found this small blue piece of glass, this ocean in my hands.

The Appalachian Sea

Once every while it returns to remind us and carry us away.

    Once it snowed three feet when we were by the river and when

It melted it also rained and so the river doubled up and

    Tripled like it had its children on its back, its mother

Too and the water plowed down trees alongside and covered

    The road and rose up so high it just about touched the under

Girders of the Rt. 7 bridge that shook from the force and all

    The people parking there to look and point as four of us

For no reason, for fun and drunkenness and being young,

    Climbed in a little boat with a tiny engine and zipped through

The pine-tops in the high water of the current's edge and trailers

    Meanwhile tipped end-over-end in the waters, RVs, picnic

Tables, fifty-gallon drums of who knows what and when

    We turned back against the current to go the mile home we

Kept tipping toward the middle of the water and it pulled us out

    Into the ferocity of an ocean at the middle, an ocean at storm,

The waves' forces trying to take us down to the rocks below

    While we kept to the edges best we could, and you thought, oh

This is how I die, I get it now, just like that, and all the ghosts

    In the river go *yeah this is how, this is how* as they gathered

Beside the boat to show us the way down and so when Bill

    Got us to land in silence we walked the rest of the way

And when the water finally left, it left a brook trout a foot long

    Bright in a pool by the mailbox and we caught it and freed it

In the pond, and insects covered our windows, and snakes

   Awake from their winter sleep coiled in the trees bewildered

To rest away from the cold waves of the river filling the earth

   With water like it was hollowed out, the molten core of it

All sizzling and going out, steam rising on the mountain as fog.

Of Cabinetmakers and Caterpillars

The gigantic fat caterpillars on the catalpa tree
   Moved and writhed like green baby dragons
On every leaf and you could hear them chewing
   They were so many and you could say hey to your
Friend Todd busy inside the barn and call him out
   To see and sure enough he'd come out to the catalpa
Just behind the silo and say *what, what* and then
   Holy shit as he took his index finger and started
To rub the back of the fattest green caterpillar
   You've ever seen and say *hey there fatty, you're*
Just a green hunk of pudge aren't you and yes
   I am, I am the fattest hunk of pudge you've ever
Seen and I'm going to eat this tree down to nothing
   Just you watch and while he keeps the conversation
Going on both sides he rubs smooth the spiky
   Hairs on the back of the thing now bucking under
His finger, the broad leaf leaping up and down—
   So the great moth caterpillar, a winder of silk,
Endures our wonder, patiently waiting for it to end.
   When his wingspan comes he'll have only a week
To live flying and falling through the night air like
   A windblown image of magnificence without
Equal. Until then there is work to do. Will Todd
   Go back inside and polish that mahogany table?

Yes he will. Am I going to hear the hammer and

    The saws and turn the finial of a pine clock and

Remember this tree and do we live toward loss

    And never understand? Oh yeah, yeah we do.

A Fool on the Earth

If the trees can sense a person walking by
   They'd know you as a familiar, a man or danger
As they know all men as a danger. With our
   Walking sticks and our campfires and our minds
Like axes and the long strings of words we set
   Fire to or screams. They would know us as we are:
A danger to all, even to ourselves. In art, the nobility
   Of man, his resourcefulness and his great love for
Someone or other is a grand subject and a final
   Judgement it seems, a redemption. Though mostly,
Really, I'm not sure. Even if our days are spent in toil
   To care for others seeking hope when there is little or
None, it's true the artist is a fool. The plumber is a fool.
   The priest, the I.T. guy, the snake-wrangler, the good
Samaritan, the murderer, the fellow just walking by,
   The mother and the father and the one who just died
In Topeka, a child born with anencephaly without a chance
   Without a brain stem, without anything except the merest
Knowledge of a fool which she takes with her to wherever and is no more.

Fishing under the Moon

For catfish, we caught an eel in the Shenandoah moving along
   Cold in the August periphery of summer and so it was
Prehistoric and writhing and white as moons in mirrors
   Or the hand of god raised to snatch at you as Mike grabbed
The head, undid the hook, and it sliced and twisted in the air
   Before it was thrown back into the dark river that goes to die
At Harpers Ferry or to change into another river, the Potomac,
   That goes to die or to change into a current of the ocean
That goes to die or to change along the coasts of everywhere
   At every time all over the world washing up, washing up
Onto the sand or crash-landing onto rocks and boulders under
   Cliffs where people stand or edge themselves nearer and nearer
Just to look down and wonder at the fall that might break our bones
   And feed the hungry flicker-fish and octopus and the squids
Floating in the depths alone, alone, only sometimes rising up
   To be glimpsed or washed on shore flattened by their own weight
And gravity pressing until we come along by accident with our
   Phones and see the great mass of squid and the great arms
Tentacled and unmoving, the thrash gone, the willowy light
   Undulations of movement gone, the sensitive beak open,
The liquid eye still alive gigantic watching us as we approach.

A Poor Man's Grave

I'm not down there anymore—
    I'm the color of the clay,
The silver in the wire
    And the last cut of hay.
Just like anyone there
    Standing among you,
I was born falling away.

After an Etching of Two Trees

Sometimes it feels like you are walking through a gate
  When you pass between two trees set closely together
So it seems they are working together for a purpose
  You cannot guess. And maybe it is good luck to go there
Between them and stop at the edge of the lake they guard
  As if crossing some threshold of blessings untold or
Maybe it is to walk unknown into the underworld. I don't
  Walk between two trees that stand together like that
Though it tempts me. The superstition and the worry
  Tempt me. My parents had a friend who lived by a lake
When I was maybe four or five and we drove to Alabama
  Every summer so they could water-ski and drink and laugh
And one day my little sister, unsteady, tipped from the boat
  And disappeared and all was quiet I remember like it was
Tuesday although a lifetime ago, and I remember my father
  Jumped in and dove down swinging his arms to find her
And eventually he did and she breathed the air we love
  And still does now. Oh my sister Lisa and my other
Younger sister Katie whom I adore, these two women
  Standing at the edge of things saying watch out you don't
Die just yet. Keep your senses or whatever it is you have left,
  The lake before us calm and serene by the by where we live.

White Orchids by the Window

In a spray and a bowl of cucumbers freshly picked
  By the open window. White orchids and a bowl
Of cucumbers by a window. I never would've guessed at
  The display of richness and of sex in the kitchen of
A friend of a friend. I was helping to move a piano
  Out from her house and into an old panel truck
To drive to his house and carry somehow up his steps
  To the living room that has a bare place on the wood floor
By a window where we are going. And this was
  Years ago now—I hardly remember her or her name or
Why she was getting rid of the piano for free, maybe
  Moving away or generosity. But I remember the tendons
Of her neck pulsing a little as she played some Chopin
  That was full of longing and I remember the white
Orchids, a cluster of seven or eight blossoms with
  Naked green stems rising up in a bend together leaning
Toward the sunlight of the window and the glass bowl of
  Cucumbers maybe eleven or twelve of them still warm
From the garden—I know because I grazed them lightly
  With my hands and then the orchids too burying my face
In the flowers before we left and my friend said what the
  Hell and she said go ahead that's alright, you go right ahead.

Of a Shooting

Death comes with his net down along the coast
   Looking for whoever is there. Fish killed in the bloom,
A girl in the near dark toying with the waves.

   A boat just over the horizon where the heart attack
Begins as tingling in the foot for the first mate who
   Lurches. And the moon is gone too, having been seen
By him. The New Moon is when he walks over here
   With his net along the coast, with a scythe in the fields
Or a hay-rake on the tractor cutting the rabbits
   In half, the fawn sleeping. Mangled by blades, lack
Of air, promises we tell each other and fail. We say
   It is natural, a part of life and I guess it is. Death
Taking and beating back what it wants saying *Mine,*
   Just hunting and gathering as ever before like
We always have, a man moving through the woods,
   A man walking slowly through a church or a school
With an automatic rifle and ammo to break down
   The door and massacre the innocents as he always has,
As we always have, a white man mostly with a gun
   Or it's his boy, no different now than in the past:
We kill as natural as we live—without any need
   Whatsoever, just the savor of it, the joy of being alive.

Thinking of Grace

Who said the landscape of your childhood is
 The landscape of your imagination? Because it has
Helped to explain the rivers and the ponds and all
 Of the sycamores inside me. Because the green
Darknesses hidden in the hay-shadow are a kind
 Of black pigment I see at night-time anywhere—
The shadow of the grasses, of roses and katydids.
 The shadows are the only things you trust when
You are alone and lost in the only way that is certain
 As a boy or a girl with sensation, with your own
Ideas of the woods or the barbed wire silver once,
 Now always red as dried blood. Everything like
Or as. Everything in between is and seems. Oh
 The child you were in the Bronx knows this. The child
In Beijing knows this—the common magic of being
 Alone and left with what you see and feel at
Once the same. Now an old man, I try to recover
 What I can of that day when I saw the ghost
Of an old lady I love walking suddenly toward me.
 It wasn't fear, Granny, it was grace and you approached.

In the Bends

Needing to walk and to escape the racket of my life,
   Needing nothing from anyone but to be out and away
Among the great sycamores three hundred years old,
   I walk gingerly for some reason, careful not to harm
Their roots or the splay of limbs above me and almost
   Always they are open at the base of the trunk as if
With a great door where I might climb in and stand,
   Hang a blanket and build a little table and chairs
And start a new life hidden from the ones I know.
   Like that boy in *My Side of the Mountain* we need
To be alone sometimes, to be the friend of a bird.
   And so life along the Shenandoah in springtime
Is like this in certain bends with old growth trees
   Standing like a colossus and a colossus and a colossus
Of an older world, three of them together like brothers
   Home from adventure or war, forces of equal power in
Their land now forgotten that was their fathers', their
   Mothers', for they were the people who ranged here,
Fishing and living among the trees and who could not stay
   Hidden enough from those of us who came a-hunting to burn
And to take and so you walk gingerly among the old sycamores
   So not to give away the secret of yourself, murderer and thief.

After the Library of Congress Burns

When it is only a story and a ruin
   Someone will remark its loss—
In conversation or pointing a finger
   At the ground, seeing perhaps
The figure of a horse flying over
   Or a woman holding a baby
In her arms, something Almost
   That is scorched into the stones.
Those random marks the fires made.

An Angel Standing in a Field

An elephant walking in a garden. A body on fire in the snow.

    The unlikeliest image from a dream happens out here

Constantly at wartime. Sometimes the zoos are opened,

    The alligators eaten, the monkeys shot for sport, the bodies

Of the enemy set fire in the snow, their coats and shoes

    Confiscated. A skeleton whispers to an angel his name,

His address in Kharkiv and the rest is not ours to know.

    What a skeleton says is one thing, what it whispers

To anyone while wearing an overcoat and being only bones

    And wishes is a secret. Maybe out walking the perimeter

Of a destroyed city or his old farmland or the deep woods

    Before they were conquered and set fire. What tenderness

It is to walk in a ruined place, an abandoned house

    With *Life* magazines strewn on the floor, a cornfield

Gone to harvest and winter snow, an old hotel burned

    Down to smoke and huge broken beams blackened

With soot. A slender woman sits on her husband's lap

    On the tractor as he mows the hay and she cannot say

Who he is anymore or her name though she likes him.

    She leans up and she whispers into his ear and he listens.

She cannot be left alone in the house anymore so she

    Rides along like this. *Please look after the people I love.*

In Praise of Slightness

There is so much drama among the living the dead must say.
  Even a butterfly on a sunflower is a matter of concern
To the blue jay and if we are creatures of struggle
  And meaning then we need drama—to understand
Anything of who we are. Like Aristotle said we need to
  See the murder, to feel the loss of the king, the death of
The child, to cry or to honk in laughter like Hogs of
  Absurdity for the catharsis, the expression of feeling
That fucks you over for days haunting you. The haunting
  Helps a little. The antichrist of my childhood swinging
His flaming sword as his horse rears up in the yard
  Out my window before sleep is just part of the plan
We have made—to see the end of ourselves, to see
  The end of the universe and for the end to be a victory
With blazing lights. Well alright, I guess. OK. Yesterday
  A wren zipped by my head and disappeared within
The hydrangeas and I hardly noticed until now how
  Lovely it was to feel the slightest breeze from its wings.

The Fox in the Sugar

I'd like to go back to that wisdom I had as a child.
  Back to the idea every field had a god, every hill
An angel, every river a spirit to guard and to speak
  With you if you are near or kind. Back to the notion
Of leaving a bowl of watermelon for the god of
  The woods, leaving a glass of wine or a fish for
The invisible. Back to walking down the road with
  A bag for trash, leaning down to pick up the cans and
The tossed wrappers. She goes slowly at the edge of
  The road for a mile a day whoever she is—I fly by
In my truck giving her some room and maybe a little
  Honk but never helping out. I don't help. Once I saw
Her walk around a dead fox killed by the speed of
  Someone like me—driving, driving everywhere too
Fast, unfeeling, hardly looking, just going and going
  Because I am more important obviously smarter,
More capable than what runs on four legs, what moves
  By bounds and the secret shadow paths of night-time,
The fox, the guardian of this cornfield that goes on
  And on and where you can smell the sugars in the air
So sweet it is the perfume of summer and there he was,
  A wild dog with red hair just standing looking in the light.

A Child's Leg with a White Shoe

I keep thinking about the lions in Washington DC
   In the zoo that my sister could hear roaring
On summer days when her windows were open,
   How far away they were from running and gazing at
Long distances or feeling the bark of trees give under
   Their climbing rather than the concrete that takes
The place of trees. In America our place in things,
   In all things earthly is disproportionate and spiders
In Guatemala, rare spiders are dying off, birds
   With green stripes and a call that would haunt
You are gone. A boy in Palestine under the tons
   Of rubble that was a high-rise, the boy who liked to
Whistle, to call to his cat, to wrestle his brother
   Also under there, the dream he had of the sea
Rising up like a green curl of words and washing
   Through the city taking him and his family in a small
Boat to what his grandfather says was heaven
   After all, a green land of olives and white clouds
In the air and lions in the hills and the people we
   Are killing every one of them now we are killing.

Of the First Sleep after a Death

Notice how the curving waves
   Of her hair lay across
The pillow and the pillow holds
   The shape of her sleeping
And the face betrays her sleeping.
   Notice the eyelashes like hay
Combed after mowing—
   Notice the forehead as calm
As the white of bones. See
   The way the line of the nose
Descends to the rested valley
   And cliffs of the upper lip.
The way the sheet luffs up
   When she moves a little
From the dream she makes up
   As she goes and all the facts
Of that kingdom blind to us.
   The way a teacup rests
In the flat paw of the bear.
   The silence of the forest
Deepening and the fleet ghost
   Of her father flying overhead.
Even the mockingbird hunched
   In a nest in the middle branch
Of the pine sleeps. We find peace.

The Recital

It was narrow in the alcove and darkened with crimson
  Swishings of taffeta and ballerinas crowded around
And rushed into the light like Roman candles and
  The odor was a fragrance—of sweat and flowers,
And I was maybe thirteen and my sister was flying out
  With the dancers into the wheeling lights they were
Making with their motions like throwing stars, like
  Lanterns spinning in the air. It was otherworldly to be
A teenager at last seated breathless in a small room
  As the dancers rushed past and was like a baptism
To float there as if in a river and not much since
  Has compared in loveliness except the Shenandoah
In spring when the blue-bells flare out and cover
  The land with that fragile seeming blue dazzle that
Darts in the eyes so it hurts the pleasure-zones deep
  In the brain. I only did cocaine once and it was
Like three cups of coffee and acid made me laugh
  And whiskey is nice for the mellow falling away
From life I love at the end of the day. But to be there
  In the alcove was better, finer. Was being lost and alert
In the trance of time passing, brushing its body against mine.

Like, As, And and *Fire*

How do you get to heaven if it doesn't exist?

    Through songs? Through lies? By dying?

Being the wish that wants and the one desire?

    Through the words we love that make us

Rich like *like, as, and* and *fire?*

    Under the moon every night in the yard,

Under the sun through the single beam

    That causes your eyes to close? Through

Dream where you are flying light and fast

    Like riding a river or being its going?

Heaven was under the Real and rose

    As we grew. Heaven was none, not ever

Ours although now I smell the brocade

    And the gold of the day in the quick

Rush of our going. The pressing of my hand

    Into your hand. The pressing of my hand

Against the coarse brick wall—the feathery

    Feeling of something that will not give, is.

How Cloud Shadow Passes over the House

It reminds me of my friend's tattoo of a buffalo,

    How it moves as the muscles move beneath.

How the indistinct tracery of water on water

    On the surface of the river makes patterns

That seem opposite and delicate compared

    To the great heave of water moving beneath.

How the changing expressions of the face

    While we sleep show subtle recognitions as

Dream moves the eyelids and the lips begin to

    Speak. The lacework of water over rock carves

Its way down hill, down the cliff leaving marks

    You can read if you know how. Like the blue marks

On the arms of a Bronze Age mummy in Syria:

    The crescent and the triangle, the lion and the tree.

I like not knowing what any of it means, not being

    My business actually at all, but I love knowing

It meant something to her, specific probably sacred.

    The pinpricks of her pain a reminder, a message.

The only tattoo I've ever considered is BORN TO DIE

    In uppercase on my chest, the O of TO going around

My nipple just above the heart. I imagine it there

    Though it is not and I like it there, even though it is not.

Half of Love

Is a bird with its throat cut, lying there motionless,

    A white duck where the snow has melted. Is loss, missing

The beloved, being without, wondering where they are, not

    Having though wanting and wanting to care for, to keep,

To protect, to hold onto. Half of love is always death.

    The gone and no-more who never come back unless

They do in dream or a photograph or the wildness of

    The mind as it suffers and they walk through the door

Again. Is them going out for groceries and the meanwhile

    When you are alone and the only evidence of them

Really is that loneliness, the what-if of never coming back.

    A dead bird always says it best, like a buzzard hit

By a truck near the carcass of a deer, or a parakeet

    At the bottom of its cage, its bright green feathers so

Lovely still my friend suddenly lifts her when he finds her,

    Lifts his dead bird to his mouth like a cigar and says—

You got a light? Love is ridiculous like this also, cannot

    Be contained, offensive and stupid and the only reason

To remain on the earth alive. The death of a bird, so

    Common, the half of love we eat often after we shoot it

From the sky. You were here with me once I remember,

    And you killed me you say. Yes love, yes I remember that day.

The Panther in the Hills

Named for the strong nets the Romans used to catch
   The wild cats and carry them back to the Colosseum to
Fight each other or men condemned to die. The panther
   Sleeping in the branches opens one eye as you walk beneath.
The panther hidden in the natural shade of three rocks
   In the hills above your house. The panther leaping.
The panther screaming like a lady's ghost out for blood
   Killing someone who probably deserves it—a cheating
Man, someone with a hatchet climbing through her
   Window. The panther eating the legs of someone, pulling
With its teeth at the sinews and cracking the bones.
   The panther peaceful only needing to eat, not trying
To scare you, only being. The panther waiting listening for
   The rabbit or the deer as they get closer until it is too late
And the graceful pounce comes to its end. The panther
   Even calm and patient in mid-air, its hair short and soft, its
Eyes like a housecat like something you could love from
   A distance in the dark, leaving it alone forever as it wishes.
The panther prowling in the nucleus of the cell, in the cages
   Of zoos, in the Divine, unseen. The panther in the garden
Sleeping in the sacred books dreaming of blood and sunlight.

Vow

At the crematorium,
    Line her coffin
With jars of honey
    So they will explode
She said, place
    Your hand again
On my forehead
    Softly, she says. Ok?
Write it down. *Ok.*

A Great Moth Like a Man in the Woods

Or something like a man about eight feet tall waiting
    For you at the side of the path and a pile of bones
In the cave at the base of the cliff and a dog on a chain
    With nothing to say, terrified. One time I saw a dead
Body beside the road, Rt. 340, a motorcyclist lying
    In the grass berm so still stillness embodied the man
Face down his legs splayed at broken angles, his bike
    Still running and a paramedic just arriving kneeled down
To him as we drove past very slowly, quieted, rubber-
    Necking. Sometimes when I'm terrified I go for a walk
In the woods or across pastures of farms I don't even
    Know, just go on moving my body in its rhythm so
My heart relaxes and keeps a steady beat my mind follows
    Always: walking to walk and never to arrive is like prayer
Or meditation and I think of the prisoner in the yard doing
    Laps like the middle-schoolers in gym class circling
The track, walking with their friends, and my wife will
    Take pepper-spray in the early morning when she walks
Our dog in case someone is there on the path waiting
    For her and always we imagine he is waiting for us
Whoever he is—ready—with large white eyes on his wings.

Of a Book of Paintings by Miles Cleveland Goodwin

I just traded a crisp two-dollar bill for a Heineken

    And am sitting by the empty silo out my window at work

Looking at a book of paintings that is like walking through

    A house in the dark glamour of the woods in the afternoon.

All blacks and greens and shadows and streaks of light

    So what you can see outside corresponds to what happens

Inside—so you know it's true—the dream of being born,

    Tumbling through unknown years of childhood remembering

Maybe a red lamp or the shape of your mother's face as

    Gospel. And the dream of carrying on until now with a number

From the Social Security Office and your body always with you

    Except for sleep and drinking. I just traded a two-dollar bill

For a Heineken and am floating a quarter-inch off the earth.

    If a person can be at home and feel at home even for a day,

She is luckier than King Henry VIII or Queen Elizabeth,

    More powerful and happier. For now by the silo in the June

Clarity of sunlight at 3 PM, my home is here in this place

    Where cows wander and corn grows and the imagination,

A funnel of turning, rises with black wings inside me.

    Always it sets me back down again in the whorl

Of its passage through the land where we are busy seeing

    Things that might save us even for a second from the grave.

In Spoons and Cups of Water

How oppressive it is sometimes to be seen, looked at,
     Gazed upon, considered and watched when you
Only want to be at the side of the mountain and never
     On top, to be a few slashes of color in the audience
In *The Circus* by Chagall and never the artist
     On the trapeze or the horse in the air and yet
There we are at the center of our lives like movie stars.
     Let me be a whole galaxy of light we'll never see
Going on forever, be the recognition of delight
     And not the laughter, the floor that is always
A secret uncounted part of the stairs. Every
     Painting sees me and most do not care, every
Song hears me out here, everyone we encounter
     In the elevator sees you without exactly looking.
The sky doesn't look upon us though it feels that way.
     Think of the one in solitary confinement in prison
With no one to see although watched on closed circuit tv,
     Left to die without looking upon another. My face is pink
And symmetrical with a gray beard rough as lace and
     I keep thinking of yours, whoever you are, and your lashes
And the lines of your nose and how it is tenderness always
     To behold your mother there in spoons and cups of water.

For the Lady in the Pines

Rolling in the silver moving in the dark,
   The river rises in the valley to a sea
And no one comes to save her,
   So she swims a minute through
Her window out among the trees
   Where the owl sings and calls as ever
Though she can't hear above the roar
   Of waves that was a while ago only
The land she knows. It changes and
   We go—the river rising in the valley
To a sea, the one where we come from
   Where the waves are taking her
Rolling in the silver moving in the dark.

Walking in a Graveyard in West Virginia

To stand in awe of something is enough sometimes—
   To be dumbstruck by beauty, helpless with wonder
Is more than I've ever asked of being here: the green
   Of the green cemetery grass in March when the trees
Are still mostly barren. The green essence of the blades
   All together pointing at the sky or falling over leaning
On each other, the darkness of green mixed with
   The unbelievable shimmer and invisible light from the sun
Drenching the white stones with a kind of illumination
   So the graves glow in the late morning. It's enough to
Come here as a living man who does not need gods as
   Much anymore. A living man with crocus flowers and
Daffodils held in a cluster with a rubber band. This gift
   For the dead. All the stones flower-decked and scrubbed
With light this month. Skull after skull looking up or turned
   To the side just below me, my skull carried carefully
On my neck bones through the first full day of Spring
   That feels lucky like a ladder has been dropped and
We should climb, all of us now out of winter for good
   Although it's ok we cannot. And to die eventually. To
Stand in awe that we cannot and carry flowers is enough.

Of Queen Anne's Lace along the River

At the far edge of the monastery's pasture that rolls gently
   To the Shenandoah and then drops like a cliff down
To water about twelve feet suddenly below the Holsteins,
   You got to clamber up out of the riverbed and hold
Tree roots and pull the vines and Queen Anne's lace to
   Get up out of the water if you have been swimming
Or walking out on the rocks and the ripples there. And so
   I've trespassed up that boundary to lie in the scraggle
Just to rest. To smell the wall of earth I am ascending
   Awkward as ever—to smell the lines of honeysuckle
Like apples green in your hands, to smell the little shells
   From the sea this was a million years ago—the cliff dotted
With fragile curlicues of something ancient and the veils
   And doilies of the lace of wild carrot named for a queen
Of England in the eighteenth century who is now lost
   To bone fragments, moss, and a gown of minerals dark
As this wall of earth I lean on resting—her body gone
   To three hundred years, her flowers making the riverside
Elegant though the books say they only grow in waste
   Places and abandoned fields and these are my favorite
Reaches to rest in and to breathe after swimming in the river
   While the monks sing their good-night songs about a mile away
And you can hear the final bells of the evening and live a while
   Longer if you like they say. Live a while longer if you like they say.

Acknowledgments

The poem "Of the First Sleep after a Death" was first published with a different title by *Poetry International* and included in the chapbook *Songs for the Carry-On,* published by Q Avenue Press.

~~~~~~~~~~

Great thanks to the American painter Miles Cleveland Goodwin, whose work directly inspired at least forty of these poems and whose genius renewed my imagination.

Thanks to Terrance Hayes for reading the first draft of this work and guiding me forward, and thanks to Dave Smith for reading every draft with such patience. Thank you both for encouraging me with friendship and good counsel.

Thanks to Russ Bahorsky and Susan Varnot for your incisive clear reading of this book when I was most stuck and for your generosity and friendship, which for thirty years have deepened my sense of poetry. Thanks to Ross Gay, Curtis Bauer, and Patrick Rosal, my comrades.

Thank you to Senta Larsen for your encouragement from far away, and thank you to Glenn Taylor and Brian Brodeur for good advice and abiding with me in conversation and friendship as I wrote this book. Thanks also to everyone at Nick Greer Antique Conservation for your patience and encouragement. In particular, thank you to Todd Hardy, Billy Chadduck and Chris Mazza.

Thank you to John Mark Power and Frank Sheridan for our conversations about poetry and music and gods and mountains as I wrote these poems.

Thank you to my parents and my sisters for love and always looking forward with me, and thanks always to Kathleen and Isabella and Elijah for being here with me and making everything near beloved.

Thank you to Norman Dubie for your poetry and our night-walks in the desert.

www.ingramcontent.com/pod-product-compliance
Lightning Source LLC
Chambersburg PA
CBHW050906240625
PP16682700001B/1